The Last Two Alive!

by

Alfred Coppel

Double9 BOOKS

The Last Two Alive!

by Alfred Coppel

ISBN: 978-93-63051-43-0

Published by

DOUBLE 9 BOOKS

2/13-B, Ansari Road
Daryaganj, New Delhi – 110002
info@double9books.com
www.double9books.com
Tel. 011-40042856

ABOUT THE AUTHOR

Alfred Coppel, a prolific author of science fiction and adventure novels, crafted his masterpiece "The Last Two Alive!" as a gripping tale of survival and human resilience in the face of cataclysmic disaster. Set against the backdrop of a post-apocalyptic world, Coppel intricately weaves together the harrowing journey of the last two survivors as they navigate the desolate landscape and confront the challenges of rebuilding civilization. In "The Last Two Alive!", Coppel showcases his mastery of storytelling, immersing readers in a world of suspense, danger, and hope. Through vivid descriptions and compelling character development, he brings to life the struggles and triumphs of the protagonists as they strive to overcome seemingly insurmountable odds. With its gripping narrative and thought-provoking themes, "The Last Two Alive!" stands as a testament to Coppel's skill as a writer and his ability to captivate readers with tales of adventure and survival. Through his timeless masterpiece, Coppel invites readers to ponder the resilience of the human spirit and the enduring power of hope in the face of adversity.

CONTENTS

THE LAST TWO ALIVE!

The verdict, thought Aram Jerrold wearily, would be death. The Supreme Council itself would demand it. He had rebelled against the Tetrarchy—rebelled senselessly, desperately, without hope of success or escape—and the reckoning had come. The Government of the Thirty Suns would demand his life ... more, if the science of the Security Police were up to it. Aram repressed a shudder. He knew that science well. No one rose to a position of command in the Thirty Suns Navy or to membership in the Executive Committee of the Tetrarchy without respect for the methods of the dread Greens.

The courtroom was dark, a pattern of sombre hues calculated to impress a prisoner with the futility of hope. It had been weeks since Jerrold had seen the sun. Weeks of endless interrogation and repeated narcosynthesis. He had been shunted from Bureau to Bureau, from Department to Department, each set of cogs in the vast governmental machinery of the Terminus probing him for evidence of sabotage or rebellion within its own structure. He had been badgered, beaten, drugged and threatened. Now, at last, the end of the ordeal seemed near. There remained only the sentence of death to be passed—the method and place decided upon—and it would be done with. The ponderous bureaucracy of the Tetrarchy had wrung him dry, and now it prepared to cast him aside, satisfied that his rebellion was a purely personal aberration and not part of a widespread plot against the stability of galactic tyranny.

The drugs had clouded his vision, giving a nightmare mistiness to the shadowy courtroom. Jerrold could see that the room was empty but for the guards and clerks and the black-masked tribunes. It would not do, of course, to let the people know that one of the chosen masters—a member of the Executive Committee—had suddenly become an insubordinate rebel and traitor.

Behind him a door opened, splitting the gloom with a fleeting wedge of light. The wedge vanished and Aram Jerrold heard again the light, crisp footsteps. He knew without looking that it was Deve Jennet. She had been in the courtroom every day, giving testimony, slamming doors in his face.

Doors that might possibly have led to freedom. Every day she had driven another rivet into the chains of evidence that bound him, methodically, deliberately.

She passed by him without turning her head and took a seat near the tribune's dais. Jerrold stared at her through the mist that swam sickeningly before his eyes. Dimly, the memory of her as she had been before this nightmare came to him. He remembered her, soft and yielding in his arms through the long nights of Terminus. Nights filled with tenderness and longing talk of freedom for the two of them somewhere beyond the stars.

This was the same woman, but changed. The lustrous dark eyes were the same, and the full lips. The same pale hair and slim body. But it sat encased in a severely cut uniform, all femininity gone from it. The uniform was green. The hated color of the Security Police....

Jerrold had heard again all the words that he had spoken to her through those nights. Only this time the words had been retold to three masked judges and their clerk. This time, the words had had a ring of doom.

At first Aram had suffered the tortures of the damned wondering why Deve had betrayed him. He had known well enough her high connections in the Supreme Council and he had known that she served as a member of the Greens. But he had imagined that she loved him, and he had been stupid enough to trust her. Now, after weeks of ordeal, it seemed to matter no longer. Jerrold wanted only to rest.

On the dais, one of the black-masked figures was speaking. Aram leaned forward painfully to catch what was being said.

"This court wishes to go on record as favoring a severe reprimand for the Bureau of Psychometrics personnel involved in the testing of Aram Jerrold. His inherent instability should have been uncovered long before he was appointed to the Executive Committee. Only the chance use of a mental probe on him—at the request of the Security Police—" he nodded toward Deve Jennet, "—prevented serious inconvenience to the Government of the Thirty Suns. Such negligence cannot be tolerated in so vital a Bureau."

He paused while the clerk recorded his remarks, then continued: "Aram Jerrold, you have been convicted of treason against the Government of the Thirty Suns. You have been proved guilty of attempting to use your position as an officer of the Thirty Suns Navy to steal a spacecraft and escape from the dominance of your government. You have disgraced your uniform and your high office as a member of the Executive Committee of the Supreme Council of the Government of the Thirty Suns—" The hooded man rolled the sonorous phrases off his tongue with obvious relish. "Have you anything to say before the sentence of the court is passed?"

Jerrold looked at Deve Jennet. She sat motionless, her body tense in the green Police uniform. It was hard for Jerrold to speak. The druggings and violent interrogations had left him weak. Yet a spark of rebellion remained. Enough to lash out against his tormentors for one last time.

"I ... I want only to say," he began thickly, "that ... what I have done ... I would do again, gladly. I was sick of oppression ... tired of not ... daring even to think a thought of my own. Sick of pompous bureaucratic tyranny...." Jerrold drew a shuddering breath. "The Tetrarchy rules thirty star-systems ... but thirty star systems are not the Universe. Somewhere, I thought ... there must be freedom. My crime ... was *failure* ... nothing more!"

"Enough!" The tribune's voice shook with sudden anger. "This court is not convened to listen to treasonous tirades! The clerk will strike the prisoner's remarks from the record!"

Darkness flickered momentarily at the edges of Jerrold's field of vision. He felt spent by his effort at defiance. He forced himself to stand erect.

"The sentencing will proceed!"

"The prisoner will face the Standard!" intoned the clerk.

Aram raised his eyes to the hated symbol on the wall behind the judges' dais. Long habit made him square his shoulders under the tattered remains of his blue uniform. He stared up at the Standard of the Tetrarchy's Spaceship and Sun, despising everything it stood for.

"Aram Jerrold, traitor and rebel: you are sentenced by this court to death by slow disintegration! For the safety of the Tetrarchy!"

The words fell like stones from the lips of the masked tribune into the fragile silence of the vaulted chamber.

In spite of himself, Jerrold flinched. Sometimes men survived weeks of torment under the cancerous rays of the disintegrators....

One of the judges spoke in low tones to his colleagues.

"We have received a request from Kaidor V, gentlemen. Provincial Governor Santane asks that this sentence be commuted to life imprisonment on Kaidor V so that the prisoner may be used in some experimental work now in progress there."

Aram could feel his stomach muscles tightening and the weakness seeping into his knees. The disintegrators would be preferable to becoming an experimental animal on Kaidor V. The Kaidor province was the farthest of the Thirty Suns, and the arsenal of the Tetrarchy. The ghastliest of the Tetrarchy's weapons came from Kaidor, and they had to be tested there ... on living men.

"It seems," muttered one of the tribunes pettishly, "that every time a naval officer is convicted of anything a request comes through from Kaidor that he be turned over to Santane. One would imagine Governor Santane is building a navy!" He shuffled the papers before him while the others waited. "Still," he continued thoughtfully, "it would be politically unwise to execute this prisoner here on Terminus. The spacemen of his command are based here and there is no point in stirring up trouble in the Fleet... I am inclined to recommend acceptance of this offer to take him off our hands."

"*Objection, sirs!*" Jerrold looked about to see that Deve Jennet was on her feet, addressing the members of the tribunal.

"As you know, sirs," she was saying crisply, "I have the good fortune to be one of the lesser members of the Executive Committee in my office as liaison officer from Security. I feel it only fair to warn you that the Supreme Council would be extremely displeased if this prisoner should escape with his life. It is felt that an example must be made of him. If it is unwise to carry out the sentence here on Terminus, I will be happy to arrange a transfer to Atmion IV. On the Green planet there will be no possibility of trouble by Fleet members. I must insist that you accede to the wishes of the Council. Aram Jerrold must die in the disintegrators. No other course of action will be acceptable to the Supreme Council!"

The three judges conferred among themselves and then the senior spoke again. The tone of his voice indicated all too well the awe in which the Supreme Council and all its appendages was held by members of the Judicial Department of the Thirty Suns Government.

"This court was not aware that the Supreme Council had any special desires concerning the disposition of this case. Had it been known to us earlier, we would not have considered even for a moment the request of Provincial Governor Santane."

"The Supreme Council, gentlemen," returned Deve Jennet stiffly, "*has* an interest in this case, as I have indicated to you. It has been communicated to you in the proper time and form. I await your action on it."

"Of course, Leader Jennet, of course. It was not our intention to question the policies of the Council!" The judge signalled the guards.

"Aram Jerrold is hereby remanded to the custody of the Security Police, to be transported by first available spaceship to Atmion IV, there to be put to death in the manner prescribed by Directive 25-A-38 governing Execution of Convicted Persons Above the Rank of Commander. Remove the prisoner!"

Aram passed near Deve Jennet as she replied: "It will be so reported, gentlemen." And then looking somberly at Jerrold she added, "I myself will go to Atmion IV to see to it that this prisoner is accorded the treatment he deserves."

Aram stumbled out of the courtroom under guard. Deve's final words rang strangely in his ears, a perplexing threnody of the dreams they had shared in the hazy past. He had the odd feeling that in spite of the things that had passed, the end was not yet....

Of the flight out to Atmion, Jerrold remembered almost nothing. The iron determination that had kept him on his feet during the last days of his trial failed him at last and the reaction of the druggings he had suffered hit him ... hard. He writhed in the agonies of addiction for the duration of the trip out from Terminus. He knew vaguely that he lay in the prison ship's infirmary, strapped to a bunk. The discomforts of acceleration and the shift into second-stage flight above light speed added themselves to his tortures and filled his nightmares with nauseating spectres. For two weeks Jerrold went through sheer hell as his drug-saturated system screamed for more narcotics. None were given.

By the time the huge prison ship touched down on the dread world of the Greens, Aram Jerrold was on his way back. Spent, weak and emaciated, he heard the landing alarms and knew that he would live to face the disintegrators.

Atmion IV, the only habitable planet of a star-system bizarre and hateful! Three suns in the smoky sky, air that tasted of brimstone and ashes. Heavy, deadening gravity. A world of hot rain that fell daily out of the hazy cloud canopy, a desert at periaston and quagmire at apastron. Barren ground and a turbulent, sulphuric sea.

The three suns blazed through the overcast as the prison ship settled into the steaming mud that was the spaceport. Scalding rain sluiced down the long flanks of the vessel, corrosive and fetid.

Aram Jerrold knew of Atmion IV. No officer in the Fleet did not. It was a foul planet, a world unwanted by any of the many Bureaus, and as such the perfect prison world. The planet of the Greens. On all its vast hulk there was only one settlement. The Green Fortress. Political exiles and condemned prisoners from all over the Tetrarchy of the Thirty Suns were brought to the Fortress on Atmion IV. None ever returned.

Aram remembered that Atmion lay in the Twenty Ninth Decant, only four light years from Kaidor on the very periphery of the Tetrarchy. These were the outpost systems, the suns far from mighty Terminus and the center of the teeming life of the galaxy. These were the hinterlands of empire, sullen, unknown, unwanted.

The Green Fortress proper stood on a high crag, etched against the smoky grey of Atmion IV's eternal overcast. Standing in the open port of the prison ship, Jerrold could see the black bulk of the turreted stronghold through the curtain of driving rain. The spaceport was a sea of mud that still boiled in places from the heat of the great starship's landing jets.

Chained in a long line, the human cargo of the vessel was herded through the rain and mud toward an electrified wire enclosure. Aram smiled wryly at that evidence of "Security." What need was there for it on this world? Where could a prisoner go if he should find himself on the other side of the wire barrier? It was likely, Jerrold thought, that there was a Directive on it from Terminus, and that accounted for the electrified wire.

He estimated that there were perhaps nine hundred men and women in the human chain that stretched from the starship to the long reception buildings within the enclosure. The chaff of heterodoxy—cast off by the single-track machinery of galactic bureaucracy.

The Greens drove the sodden prisoners through the gates without rancor or interest. It was as though the prisoners had ceased to be human once they crossed the line that excluded them from the society of free men.

Inside the long, draughty shelters, the prisoners were stripped naked, men and women alike, run through cleansing water jets, dried, clothed and photographed. Then they were broken into groups and registered by Greens sitting in armored cubicles within the walls. There was a machine-like efficiency to the bureaucratic procedure on this level. Aram Jerrold had the impression that the operation would continue to run by sheer momentum should higher authority suddenly try to halt it....

Jerrold presented himself before a Green of about forty, a man with a thin, tired face and colorless eyes, who codified the information given him, looking up at the prisoner with no apparent interest. Quite abruptly, he emerged from his cubicle, signalling another Green to take his place.

"You," he said to Aram; "come with me."

Jerrold followed the Green out of the reception building and out into the rain. For a wild moment, Aram had the impulse to try an escape, but the thought died stillborn. Escape was plainly impossible. There was simply no place to go—even if he could shake free of his guard and the others stationed about the enclosure. The prison ship was being refuelled a short distance from the reception pen, but the valves were closed and guarded.

Presently Jerrold and his guide reached a shaft imbedded in the side of the crag, atop which sat the grim Fortress. Aram turned his eyes upward. The great, bastioned stronghold seemed to crouch on the crest of the cliff. On the highest turret, a green banner emblazoned with a golden Spaceship and Sun hung sodden and limp in the falling rain.

With no hesitation, the Green stationed at the guard-post by the shaft entrance signalled Aram and his guide through. There was a short walk up a spiralling ramp and then they stood before what appeared to be simply a blank wall. Jerrold stared in perplexity as his guard took a bit of metal from his tunic and held it to the wall.

"Isotope," said the guard shortly, "It acts as a key to the scanner ... below."

Before Aram could question him, the section of wall slid back soundlessly and they stepped into a tubecar. Quickly, the Green set up a complicated series of stops on the tubecar controls and the vehicle started downward with a rush.

Aram clutched at the man for support. Something was not as it should be. Then, quite suddenly, he realized what it was. The tubecar was travelling *down* ... and the Fortress lay above!

"Where are we going?" he asked cautiously.

The Green shook his head.

"Aren't the condemned cells above in the Fortress?"

"Be quiet. Talk is dangerous!"

"But...."

"Be quiet," the Green said again. "You'll understand soon enough. We have to be careful. Not all of us here are of the Group." He turned his back on Jerrold.

Aram's head was spinning. What was there on Atmion that a Green need fear? And what was this ... Group?

With a wisdom born of his long imprisonment, Aram Jerrold decided to hold his peace. What would be would be, and it was becoming increasingly plain that he was about to learn of things that he had not dreamed existed.

After what seemed to be an interminable period, the tubecar began to slow. The hum of atomics died and the car came to a stop. They must be well below the level of the Fortress now, reflected Jerrold, and very likely under the sea. The panels slid away and in front of them stretched a long white corridor lighted by dim bulbs set in the curved ceiling.

"There are miles of tubeways down here," said the guard, "and only the isotope key gives entrance. The central pattern on the tubecar has been altered, too ... for the safety of the Group. Follow me."

At the end of the corridor, a steelite door barred further progress. The Green produced his isotope key again and touched it to the metal.

"A word of advice," he said to Jerrold coolly. "Listen and believe. A great many risks have been taken and a vast amount of work done to bring you this far."

He leaned forward and shoved the metal door open. Within lay a brightly lit chamber. The glare of it hurt Jerrold's eyes and he stood a moment, blinking on the threshold. Slowly, as his eyes accustomed themselves to the light, Aram became aware of a group of men and women who watched him impassively. There were a few in Fleet uniform. One or two of them casual acquaintances he had thought lost in space or imprisoned by the Greens. There were others in prison garb, and here and there he could see the dread color of the Security Police. His heart began to pound. Another trap? But why?

One slight figure in green stood a little apart, watching him through shadowed eyes. Jerrold felt the breath catch in his throat.

It was Deve Jennet!

With a cry Deve ran to him. Jerrold felt a surge of mixed fury and desire. Almost defensively, he lifted his hand and struck Deve across the face.

She gasped and stepped back, eyes suddenly bright with tears, a thin streak of blood marking her pale face. The gathered strangers muttered angrily. Aram turned to stare at them; his face set and grim. Anger was pulsing within him, a deep, consuming anger born of the tortures he had suffered—he looked at the stunned girl—because of *her*.

"Oh, Aram ... what have they done to you?" whispered Deve.

"What have *they* done to me?" he asked thickly. "*They?* Now tell me you had no part in it!" He was hemmed in, lost in a sea of treachery and formless dangers. For a few moments he had dared to let himself hope...! And this was the end of it. Deve again. And another trap! "What more do you want from me? Is this just entertainment for you? To raise my hopes and then step on them again? Maybe you'd like to open my veins and have a drink of my blood?"

"Aram ... *stop it!*"

"You lying, cheating wench! Was it you that brought me to the Fortress? Was it you that spilled all my stupid dreams to those black ghouls who tried me?" he asked bitterly.

"Yes! Yes, it was me!" sobbed Deve, "but can you listen to me? Aram, I beg you! Listen to me!"

Aram felt some of the rage draining out of him. He stared at Deve in confusion. There were tears streaking her face. There was no reason for her to cry now, he thought heavily. Her job was done. Done well.

"I had to do it that way, Aram. You can't know how I've suffered for you ... every minute of the time. But it had to be done, I swear it! There was no other way I could get you here to the Group! If I had let you go your own way, you'd have been killed, Aram. I'd have died with you gladly, but there are other things that must be done. And we can live, Aram! Do you understand me? We can live!"

Jerrold looked about him. The group had gathered around him. Someone said: "Listen to Deve Jennet, Jerrold!"

Dave stepped close to him again, her face upturned. He felt again the old desire for her, even here—now. Did it matter that she had betrayed him? Did anything matter any more to him? The last ebb of fury flowed out of him, leaving him silent and relaxed at last. If this was a trap ... what did it matter? He had nothing to lose now.

He realized quite suddenly then that he wanted very much to believe what Deve said. He wanted it so badly that he reacted defensively, not daring to let himself be hurt by her again. Very cautiously, he let down the barriers that he had erected against her since the very first day of the trial when he had known for the first time that she had been his betrayer.

Deve sensed the change in him and laid a hand on his arm. "You ... you will listen now?" she asked quietly.

Aram nodded, his eyes fixed on her face. The bruise on her lips was dark and painful looking.

"I heard of your arrest the day it happened, Aram," she said. "I knew what the end of it would be if they could find no real evidence against you—you'd have been subjected to an extensive mental probing that would have left you ... an ... an idiot. That's true. You know it is."

Aram nodded agreement.

"You would have been lost to *us*," Deve said, "and Aram, we need you! Need you desperately!"

Aram looked about him in confusion. Still weak from his bout with the drugs, he was having difficulty marshalling his thoughts.

"Who are you people?" he demanded. "*What* are you?"

A grizzled naval officer stepped forward. Aram recognized him as Kant Mikal, recorded in the headquarters of the Thirty Suns Navy as having been lost in space two years earlier while on a routine exploration into the Thirtieth Decant.

"We have no name, other than 'the Group,'" he said simply. "We have as our purpose the prevention of a disastrous war ... possibly even the destruction of civilization as we have known it."

"You don't make any sense," Jerrold said confusedly. "What is there in the galaxy that can threaten the Tetrarchy with a war such as you describe?"

"There is a very real and present danger, Aram Jerrold," Mikal said flatly. "*Santane....*"

Aram felt a chilling premonition. Santane again. He remembered the testy words of the black judge who had condemned him: "One would think Santane were building a fleet...."

Mikal seemed to read his thoughts. "Yes," he said, "Provincial Governor Santane."

"I don't ask you to join us for the sake of the Tetrarchy, Aram," pleaded Deve Jennet earnestly, "or because of any personal relationship between you and me. If the Thirty Suns Government knew of the Group, and of the manipulations we've performed to get equipment and personnel for our mission, not one of us would be left alive by the Greens. We've penetrated the highest circles, we've subverted loyal people. We've used every trick and subterfuge to get the men and women we need out here without giving away our secret." She smiled ruefully. "We've even had men arrested and condemned so that we could gather them here on Atmion IV...."

Aram felt a terrible load being lifted from his shoulders. No matter what happened next, it was good to know that Deve had not betrayed him as he had thought.

"The Tetrarchy would not allow the existence of such a unit as the Group for a moment. Every hour that passes increases our danger. But we must finish our mission, Aram; we can do nothing else!" Deve said fervently.

"If Santane overthrows the Tetrarchy," said Kant Mikal bleakly, "the dark ages will descend. The man is mad for power, cruel and intelligent enough to hold it."

Aram thought swiftly. Santane was a relative unknown back on Terminus, was merely one of the thirty civil servants that held the Governorships of the Thirty star-systems making up the Tetrarchy. The Tetrarchy was a tyrannous bureaucracy ... but at least it was not a one-man government. As bad as it was, Santane's iron hand would be infinitely worse.

"But how," protested Jerrold. "With what? How can Santane hope to withstand the whole of the Tetrarchy's power?"

"As you have guessed," Mikal said, "he is building a fleet; new construction and better than anything in the Thirty Suns Navy. However, if it were only that, there would be no real need for us to interfere. The Fleet is antiquated, as you know, but able to muster a force of more than ten thousand first line battlecraft. No matter how good Santane's ships might be, they could not handle an attack by that kind of numbers. The Kaidor system would take a terrible beating, and most probably Kaidor V would be bombed to rubble. That would be the end of it. The destruction would be strictly localized in the Thirtieth Decant. But there is, unfortunately more ... much more."

"Aram," exclaimed Deve, "it's horrible!"

"Santane has developed interstellar guided missiles, Jerrold," said Kant Mikal. "Faster than any Fleet vessel and impossible to intercept. But that isn't the worst of it. It's the stuff he has developed for these missiles to carry...."

"Biological weapon?" asked Aram with a sinking feeling in his heart.

Mikal nodded. "Follow me," he said.

Aram Jerrold followed the grizzled naval officer into an antechamber. With Deve Jennet at his side he let Mikal lead him down a narrow, zig-zagging ramp into a stone room below the meeting hall. The place was dimly lit and there was a smell in the air that reminded Aram of a zoological garden. A strong wire mesh had been stretched across the room to divide it roughly into two sections. In the corner of the interior division, a figure squatted, gnawing on a piece of bone. The sound of its teeth scraping the bits of flesh off the shank made Aram shudder.

Mikal led him up to the wire.

"That," he said, "was a man. Santane's weapon did what you see there."

Jerrold's stomach muscles knotted. The figure in the cage was roughly human, but it squatted on greatly foreshortened hams and waved long, hairy arms at them angrily. The forehead sloped back from a face completely bestial, and as Aram stood there, sickened and fascinated, the hirsute apparition flung the chewed bone at him and bared its fangs in a blood-chilling howl.

Aram turned away, white-faced. "Is ... is there no cure for this thing?" he asked.

Mikal shook his head. "We have been able to develop none. This was an agent of ours who was taken on Kaidor IV by Santane's raiders. We tried to establish a surveillance point there and failed—the planet is hardly livable—and Santane has been able to maintain a very complete coverage of the two planets nearest his capital. The inoculation was made on Kaidor V, and Santane sent him back here, thinking him an agent of the Greens. He is laying the foundations of his psychological attack, you see. A few cases like this, and then the shocker—the announcement that every planet in the Thirty Suns can expect an attack by guided missiles loaded with that virus unless his demands are acceded to."

"But surely there must be a specific for this thing," pursued Aram. "It would be valueless as a weapon unless there is."

"The virus attacks the higher cerebral centers first," explained Mikal. "Then the endocrine balance. First memory goes. Our medical people believe that Santane *has* an antidote for this thing, but in very limited amounts. They tell me that if caught soon enough, it can be stopped. But within hours after infection permanent damage to the higher nervous system is done. They suspect that even if a very small amount of serum is introduced into the body after infection, *physical* damage can be completely avoided. What the effect on the mind might be, they do not care to say. Complete loss of memory certainly. A lessening of the ability to relearn the forgotten is also probable."

The creature behind the wire howled again, plaintively now.

"Let's get out of here," breathed Deve faintly.

"You see what Santane will use to seize the Tetrarchy," Mikal went on when they were once again in the meeting hall. "He imagines that the mere threat of it will subdue the Supreme Council."

"But that's wrong!" exclaimed Aram: "The Tetrarchy will fight! There has never been a bureaucracy in the history of mankind that didn't imagine itself invincible!"

"Yes, the Tetrarchy will fight," agreed Mikal. "And a war of absolute destruction will engulf the Thirty Suns. Unless...."

"Unless what?" demanded Jerrold.

"Unless Santane can be convinced of that. Unless he can be prevailed upon to give up his ambition and content himself with being a balance for the rest of the Tetrarchy's power. Where there's one power only, tyranny results invariably. But if there are two, co-equal and autonomous, then they must compete for the favor of the people. Only in such a way can the civilization of the Thirty Suns survive, and the slavish lot of the people of the inhabited worlds be improved.

"That, then, is the purpose of the Group. We are pledged to stop—if we can—the impending struggle for power between Santane and the Tetrarchy. Savagery is the price we will pay for failure!"

In the days that followed, Aram Jerrold grew to despise the name of Santane more than he had ever despised the Tetrarchy. Deep under the turbulent sea of Atmion IV, he rested—recuperating from his ordeals and making ready for the time when the small band of peacemakers would move to forestall Santane's bid for galactic dominion.

The plan, as Kant Mikal outlined it, was simple and direct. In the colony under the sea there were forty-five men and women. These were mainly scientists and soldiers who had incurred the wrath of the Government of the Thirty Suns, though there were some, like Leader Deve Jennet of the Security Police, who carried on a double existence on Atmion IV, living both above in the Green Fortress and in the tunnels....

Of the more than three thousand Greens stationed on the prison planet, some fifty knew of the Group, and of the fifty, perhaps ten had access to the secret quarters. These Greens, at great personal risk, supplied the scientists and workers of the Group with the materials needed for their medical and physical researches.

A falsified report of Aram Jerrold's death under the disintegrators was sent to Terminus under the personal cachet of Leader Deve Jennet of the Security Police; so for the first time in many weeks Aram had a semblance of peace.

Mikal's plan was for the Group to divide into two units. One, the larger of the two, would go—at the proper time—to Kaidor V, there to establish contact with the Provincial Governor and try by any means to dissuade him from his plan to defy the Thirty Suns Government. There were several among the Group who felt that such an approach to Santane would succeed where harsher methods might well fail in the face of the Thirtieth Decant's hidden power. It was Mikal's plan to lead this delegation himself in a starship now being fitted in the central pit of the tunnel maze.

But Kant Mikal did not delude himself that Santane could be won by arguments. Another expedition to the Kaidor Sun would be dispatched at the same time. A small two-man destroyer that had been rendered—Mikal claimed—"undetectable," would leave the Atmion system with the larger vessel and land on Kaidor III, a planet uninhabited save for a few bands of degenerated experimental subjects dumped there by Santane's biological ecologists. Mikal took care to point out that Kaidor III had two large land-masses, and the landing by the two members of the Group selected for that duty would be made on the land-mass unoccupied by the unfortunate subhumans.

This expedition would remain on Kaidor III to await word from the first as to the success or failure of the Group's plan. Failing to hear from them, or hearing of failure, the small ship would proceed to Kaidor V and try to wrest the secret of the virus weapon from Santane. Plainly enough, the second expedition into the Thirtieth Decant would be a last, spasmodic attempt to save something from the ruins of galactic war. That phrase stayed with Jerrold as he listened to Kant Mikal. *To save something from the ruins.* That, he told himself, might well be the best the Group could accomplish with their meager resources.

During the hours that Deve was working in the Fortress, Jerrold wandered freely through the maze of underground tunnels and chambers that the Group had built. The original catacombs had been built a thousand years earlier, and the men and women of the Group had expanded and refurbished the forgotten maze to suit their purposes. Jerrold was continually amazed at what they had been able to accomplish with so little at their command and under a shroud of almost complete secrecy.

Life in the tunnels centered on the central pit—the spaceport. This, as Kant Mikal explained with considerable pride, was connected with the surface by a series of locks that emerged through the bottom of the sea in the offshore shallows down the coast from the Green Fortress. Under cover of night, a spaceship could emerge from the tunnels and lift into space without arousing the garrison of Greens who served on Atmion IV never dreaming of the quiet life beneath their feet.

Two spacecraft rested in their cradles in the pit, a medium sized merchantman, the "Star Cluster," and a Fleet scout-destroyer, "Serpent." Jerrold recognized both vessels as craft that had long ago been reported lost in space in Admiralty headquarters back on Terminus. The Serpent still carried its Fleet insigne of the Spaceship and Sun, a reminder to Aram of his former life and of the immense power of the Thirty Suns Navy. He knew only too well the position of the Group in the coming silent struggle between the galactic Tetrarchy and the rebellious Santane. They were the smallest, weakest corner in a vicious triangular madness that threatened to smash the entire civilization of the Thirty Suns.

His personal happiness at being with Deve Jennet again, and free of the haunting pain of her supposed betrayal, was mitigated by a realization of the dangers they would soon face when the Group's quixotic plan went into operation. Nor were these forebodings lessened when Kant Mikal informed him that he and Deve were the unanimous choices of the Group for the second—and secret—expedition into the Kaidor Province.

"It will be your purpose," Kant Mikal told him again, "to save something from the wreckage if all else fails...."

Aram lay comfortably under the bank of sun-lamps in the underground infirmary. The days of rest and treatment had brought him back into condition again, and he felt fit and ready for action. He had begun to chafe at the inactivity, but Kant Mikal insisted that the time to move out against Kaidor had not come, and Jerrold was forced to be content with the older man's judgment.

Deve sat with him in the infirmary, her slim body golden under the glowing lamps. Sitting near her, watching the graceful sweep of her pale hair as it brushed her shoulders, Aram was filled with a sense of well-being and contentment.

"Aram," asked Deve, "have you had time to examine the Serpent? Are you familiar with that class of ship?"

"I spent three years on Periphery Patrol with Serpent class scouts, Deve," murmured Aram sleepily. "There won't be any trouble...." He stretched himself and sat up. "But there's one thing I'd like more information on ... if I can be trusted with it."

"Aram! We trust you! You know we do ..." protested Deve.

"Kant Mikal told me the Serpent was ... undetectable. In all my years with the Fleet, I never heard of a spaceship that could not be detected."

"Avon Marsh—one of our scientists—has developed an energy shield, Aram."

"That's nothing new, Deve," said Aram. "The Fleet vessels have had them for years. They use them against attack by ray weapons of all kinds."

"But this reaches into the highest frequencies," Deve explained. "It shunts all radiation around the ship. Of course, it can't be used during second order flight above light speed, but it wouldn't be of any value then, anyway."

"You mean it shunts *all* radiation around the ship? All? Even light?" demanded Jerrold with sudden interest.

"Yes. At close observational ranges it results in a slight distortion—like a very clear lens, but—"

"Then the ship is ... invisible?" Aram asked incredulously.

Deve Jennet smiled. "Yes, among other things. And it prevents a radio echo being sent back to a detector, too."

Aram sank back thoughtfully. An invisible ship! His spaceman's mind toyed with the thought. It was like something from a naval officer's dream fantasies. A battleship so equipped could very nearly rule the plenum...! But Deve's next words cut that dream short.

"The field is so limited, though," she said, "that only a two-man scout can be equipped with it. And since the shield works two ways, the occupants of the ship are blind. Nothing outside the ship itself can be seen."

Jerrold was about to reply when Kant Mikal burst into the room. His grey hair was matted with blood, and his face was pale and drawn with pain and anxiety.

"I should have listened to you, Jerrold," he breathed heavily. "We should have moved out long ago!"

"Kant! You're hurt," cried Deve.

Mikal gestured impatiently. "It's nothing! We have to get out immediately! Get ready...!"

Jerrold and Deve were on their feet, reaching for their cloaks.

"What's happened?" asked Aram.

"The Greens have found the tunnel entrance. I think they must have caught one of our topside people with a mental probe, I don't know for sure. But there's fighting in the tube-shafts now. We have to get to the ships!"

Aram cursed. "Are there any weapons nearby?"

The grey haired officer shook his head. "None. Only the medical instruments here."

Aram ransacked the wall cabinets and produced a single small scalpel. "This will have to do," he muttered.

"If we can reach the pit," said Kant Mikal, "the steelite doors may give us enough time to get clear. They're disintegrator-resistant."

"Let's go," said Aram tensely. "Ready?"

Deve and Mikal nodded and followed him as he opened the door to the corridor and stepped out. The tunnel was deserted, but there were muffled sounds of fighting coming through the ventilators. Aram sprinted toward the pit, his bare feet soundless on the stone floor. Deve and Mikal ran silently beside him.

As they came to a turn in the tube, a single Green seemed to appear out of nowhere. Aram had a fleeting glimpse of a pistol being raised and he felt the hot, searing touch of a graze as he launched himself bodily at the man.

There was a crashing roar as the tetrol shell exploded harmlessly against the stone wall of the tunnel, sending echoes reverberating down the long passageway. Aram caught the Green in the pit of the stomach with the full force of his charge. The man doubled up painfully, dropping his weapon to the floor. Aram rolled to his feet, catlike. The Green roared with rage and lunged at him. Aram stepped under the attack and brought his two clenched fists down on the back of the man's neck. The Green staggered and spun about, catching Aram in a vise-like embrace. The policeman was huge, and as his arms closed about Aram's lighter frame, Aram could feel his ribs being crushed. His hand closed on the scalpel he had thrust into the waistband of his shorts. He raised it high and drove it hard into the man's broad back. The Green stiffened. With an incredulous expression, he released Aram and toppled to the stone floor.

Aram leaned against the wall of the tunnel, panting, sickened. His hands were red with blood. From somewhere down the tunnel came the sound of booted feet clattering on the stones. Suddenly another Green rounded the turn, an energy rifle in his hands. Aram straightened for the expected attack, but the Green stopped abruptly, his head vanishing into a red smear as another crashing roar echoed down the corridor. As he sank to the floor, Aram turned to see Kant Mikal lowering the first Green's still smoking pistol.

"Let's keep going," Mikal muttered breathlessly.

Stopping only to pick up the fallen Green's rifle, Aram, Kant Mikal and Deve ran on toward the pit.

"Will the others try to make the spaceport?" gasped Jerrold as they ran.

"There's nowhere else to go," returned Mikal simply.

The Greens had not completely occupied the tunnels, for they met no more opposition. The sounds of fighting had stopped, though, as they burst into the large chamber that housed the spacecraft, and Aram realized that the Greens were gathering their forces for an attempt to prevent the Group's escape in the vessels. Aram looked about him with a sick heart. Of the original forty-five that had been in the tunnels before the attack, only ten besides himself and Deve had reached the pit. The others, they told him, had been killed or captured by the Greens, and one of them must have been forced to tell of the spaceships and the plan of escape through the locks.

The steelite doors of the pit were closed, and the remnants of the Group straggled aboard the Star Cluster. Kant Mikal took immediate command of the ship and made ready for the perilous passage through the locks to the sea above. He laid a hand on Aram's shoulder and spoke with feeling. "This isn't the way I planned it, Jerrold, but we must do the best we can. Good luck!"

Aram helped rig the Star Cluster for flight and then stepped down onto the floor of the pit. He realized only too well, as he stood with Deve alone on the floor of the vast chamber, that they would have to wait until the heavy Star Cluster had cleared the locks before they could blast free of the cavern in the Serpent.

He helped Deve through the valve of the small scout ship and hoisted himself up, crouching in the open lock with the dead Green's energy rifle, ready to pick off the first Green to come through the door. The Greens had brought their disintegrators into play, and within minutes the door would reach its limit of endurance. The steelite panels already glowed red....

The Star Cluster lifted from its cradle with a hissing roar that set the smaller Serpent to trembling. The first lock opened above it and it was gone into the black maw of the vertical shaft, its tail-flare vanishing in the stygian darkness. The lock did not close, and Aram Jerrold breathed a silent message of thanks to Kant Mikal who had left it open to ease the Serpent's escape.

"How long will it take them to clear the remaining locks?" Jerrold asked Deve anxiously.

Deve divined his thoughts, and shook her head. "More time than it will take the Greens to cut through that door!"

Aram was struck with an idea. "The shield, Deve! The energy shield!"

For a moment hope lighted her face, but it quickly faded. "There is a time-lag when the shield is deactivated, Aram," she said. "If we use it now, we won't be able to operate the locks in time. They are radio-controlled from inside the ship and the shield stops all radiation ... both ways!"

"Then we'll ram the locks!"

"Will the ship stand it?"

"I don't know, Deve, but it's our only chance. If we can confuse them just long enough to get under way, we may make it. Show me how the shield is energized."

Deve shrugged and sat down before the control panel. Her fingers flashed lightly over the banks of switches. A low whining of generators started deep in the vitals of the small starship. Aram, watching the process, glanced through the ports at the melting steelite door of the cavern, and he was amazed to see the scene fade before his eyes into a murky grayness.

"They can't see us now," Deve Jennet said with a slow smile, "and we can't see them."

"Let's go," breathed Aram.

He hurriedly began rigging the Serpent for flight, warming the jets, energizing the pumps and aerators. He gave silent thanks for the rigid training of the Thirty Suns Navy, for his hands automatically and swiftly found the proper instruments and controls. Gyros began their ascending crescendo, whining in strident unison with the shield generators to shape a harmonic pattern that pulsed in the eardrums and set the teeth on edge. Accumulators filled slowly, relays clicked shut as the Serpent poised itself for flight.

A harsh, thumping sound made Aram Jerrold pause. He cursed bitterly and resumed his work. The Greens, of course, were not fools. They could not see the Serpent, nor, presumably, had they ever encountered an invisible craft before. But having melted down the steelite portal at last and flooded into the vast pit, they could hear the Serpent's, myriad warnings of impending takeoff, and they must have begun raking the pit with projectile fire. Some of the shots were finding the invisible Serpent, and Aram knew that the destroyer's light armor could not long withstand a shelling.

"Deve! Has Mikal had time to get the Star Cluster clear of the locks now?" Jerrold shouted at the girl over the whine of machinery.

Deve Jennet had heard the projectiles too. She nodded her head and braced herself against the navigation table. "Let's go!" she shouted back.

With pounding heart, Aram Jerrold lifted the Serpent off the floor of the pit. Blindly, he let the invisible starship nose into the open shaft above. He knew that the moment the Greens realized their quarry was gone, they would begin firing blindly up into the vertical tunnel above them. If one shot should hit the jets...! Aram shuddered. The destroyer would come hurtling down out of the shaft to smashing destruction on the floor of the pit. He held his breath and eased the power forward. The Serpent responded eagerly, leaping up the mile-long tunnel....

Ahead lay the second set of locks and then the shallows of the sea. The small starship careened upward, scraping its flanks on the smooth metal of the shaft. Aram sat frozen before the controls. A thousand questions burned in his mind, and there were no sure answers for any of them.

He couldn't be sure that Mikal had gotten the Star Cluster free. He might at this moment be driving the Serpent into the atomic tail-flare of the larger ship. He did not know whether or not the small destroyer could withstand the impact of the locks ... or the sea itself. Still, he drove the ship upward and outward, the automatics set to continue the same suicidal course should his own human hands falter or fail.

He shouted for Deve to strap herself to the deck rings near the navigation table and make ready for the impact. Time seemed to slow down to a crawling pace. The breath came harshly in his throat, and sweat coursed down his naked back. His bare feet and legs felt cold and clammy....

He was not ready when it came. The first rending screech of tearing metal filled the tiny control room and the instrument panel came smashing up to meet him. He heard a whooshing roar and the scream of protesting gyros. He heard Deve cry out as her bindings ripped loose, and then blackness seemed to splash up out of the control panel and engulf him....

Jerrold woke. His head was pounding painfully and his lips felt mashed and bruised. The strap that had held him to the pilot's seat had broken, and he lay across the instrument panel in a welter of glass shards from shattered dials. The instruments were smeared with blood ... his blood, Aram realized numbly. He put a hand to his face, and it came away sticky and red.

The atomics throbbed, and the dials told him that the Serpent was still under way. The high pitched hissing of escaping air attested to the damage, but it also told him that the ship was in space ... and clear of Atmion IV.

Jerrold got dizzily to his feet and looked about for Deve. She lay crumpled in a corner under a chart-locker, bruised and scratched by the impact of the crash. She moaned slightly as Aram picked her up and carried her to the pilot's chair.

Red alarm lights glared at him from several points on the panel, showing that five forward compartments had been crumpled and ruptured by the ramming of the locks. The pressure in the ship was low enough to add to his discomfort. Methodically, fighting off the dizziness, Aram sealed off the leaky compartments and started the aerators to build up the pressure. The greyness beyond the parts indicated that the energy shield was still operating. The Serpent was traveling in slow first-stage flight toward Kaidor, four and one half light years distant.

"Aram!"

Jerrold turned to see that Deve had opened her eyes and was staring at him, horrified. He tried to grin reassuringly at her, but his bruised lips succeeded only in grimacing grotesquely through the bloody smear of his face.

Deve got to her feet, found the surgical kit that all Fleet vessels carried and set to work mending the damage. Aram was glad to find that aside from his battered lips, he had only a long scalp cut along his hair-line where the instrument panel had tried to decapitate him. The kit contained balms and soothing anaesthetics, and presently both Deve and Jerrold were patched and cleansed of blood and dirt.

There were coveralls in the lockers, and spaceboots; and a hot drink from the robot galley added to their rising spirits. They had escaped a force of the best the Thirty Suns Government could throw against them and they were free of Atmion IV. Their ship was damaged, but serviceable ... and they were together.

Deve cut the energy shield and Aram took star-shots to reckon their position. If the Greens had chased them in spacecraft, their long flight under the shield had certainly lost the pursuit, for the space behind them toward Atmion IV was clear. The three stars of the system blazed below them and Aram pointed the ship at the spot where the yellow Kaidor Sun lay just under the range of visibility, shifting into second-stage flight. The three suns of Atmion streaked into a polychromatic blur, and the Serpent plunged through the interstellar night toward the Thirtieth Decant and the unknown.

It was a star-system of ten planets. Aram Jerrold could see clearly that, as was generally the case, one of them was a ringed giant. Under planetary first-stage drive, he brought the small starship down into the system's ecliptic plane. At a distance of one light day, as the Serpent passed the outermost planet, the energy shield was reactivated.

During the days of the trip from the Twenty Ninth Decant and the Atmion Suns, no word had come from Kant Mikal and his party aboard the Star Cluster. Both Jerrold and Deve Jennet had pondered the advisability of trying to establish contact with the larger ship, but finally they decided to maintain radio silence. Aram felt it inadvisable to risk detection of the Serpent so close to Santane's stronghold.

Instead, they resolved to stick to the original plan as outlined by Kant Mikal back on Atmion IV—landing on the third planet of the Kaidor Sun and there awaiting word from the Star Cluster. Meanwhile, Aram could attempt to repair the damage caused the Serpent by the ramming of the locks.

On a dead-reckoning course, Jerrold guided the small spaceship sunward. The peaceful pleasure of the days in space was forgotten now, forced out of his mind by the nearness of Kaidor V and its hellish spawn of destruction. Thinking of the poor creature he had seen in the tunnels back on Atmion IV, Aram was taken with a sick chill. Here, under the alien light of Kaidor Sun, the virus that had degenerated what had once been a man lay quiescent in the sleek shells of uncounted interstellar missiles, ready to leap out and away and carry its mind-destroying power to all the inhabited worlds of the Thirty Suns. Jerrold knew that the use of such a weapon would mean disaster. If war came, it would be a war of stellar giants, smashing planets and minds alike in a hideous carnival of death and savagery. The spawn of the Kaidor Sun meant ruin....

As yet, Aram reflected with faint hope, there had been no break. Provincial Governor Santane was still, as far as anyone outside the Thirtieth Decant knew, a loyal civil servant of the Thirty Suns bureaucracy. The Special Intelligence reports that clicked methodically through the Serpent's subspace communicator gave no hint of rebellion against the banner of the Spaceship and Sun in the Kaidor system. It was possible, too, thought Jerrold, that the Group under Kant Mikal could convince Santane of the folly of open defiance. But even as the thoughts formed in his mind, doubt grew. Kant Mikal had said that Santane had already stopped weapons shipments to the rest of the Thirty Suns. He had no such authority. It would take some time for an investigation to be activated through the ponderous bureaucratic procedures of the Tetrarchy, but investigation there would definitely be ... and Santane could have nothing in his mind but war with the Thirty Suns Government to have taken such a risk. Kaidor Province was the scientific arsenal of the Tetrarchy, and as such strategically valuable beyond its intrinsic worth. It would not be too difficult, Aram realized, to imagine that the man who ruled Kaidor could rule the Tetrarchy. Only it wasn't so. No one system could muster enough power to crush the Thirty Suns without being smashed to rubble itself in the process. A man who had served in a galactic Fleet could understand that. But a man who had served only as a governor could not, and *that* was the danger....

As a naval officer, Aram Jerrold knew something that Santane did not. He knew that vast navies will fight and destroy long after the hope of victory has gone.

If war came, there would *be* no victory. There would be only galactic disaster....

With the energy shield off, and under reduced power, the Serpent came down into the atmosphere of Kaidor III. The planet's satellite lay, like a crescent of silver, in the dark blue, star-flecked sky of the stratosphere.

Beneath them, the vast curving surface of the planet flattened as the starship sank lower, the mottled blues and greens and browns taking shape of oceans, islands and continents. The sky grew lighter—a pale blue—as the Serpent crossed the twilight line and slanted down toward the surface of the turbulent sea.

Scud clouds raced across the sky and light rain pattered against the ports of the slowly moving spaceship. Quite suddenly the squall passed, and the Serpent hung above a sea of brilliant blues and greens, frothed with white-caps.

Deve watched through the ports, enraptured. "Look, Aram! Look at the colors in that sea!"

Side by side they watched the play of colors in the ocean, fascinated by the swirling grace and chromatic wonder of the waves.

In the far distance lay the low silhouette of land. Jerrold let the Serpent move toward it, keel skimming the dancing white crowns of the sea.

There were a few graceful sea-birds with leathery wings and brightly plumed breasts, and there was life in the sea. Deve and Jerrold could see schools of lithe shapes flashing silver beneath the water. But the land itself was silent. The white sand of a curving beach came up out of the distance to meet them. Beyond lay green rolling hills and wooded slopes bright with flowers, and farther into the glare of the morning sun great snow-capped mountains reared their jagged spines against the blue in the sky.

"Aram ... it's beautiful!" the girl breathed. "It's the world we dreamed of finding...."

Jerrold remembered the nights they had shared back on mighty Terminus. He recalled their idle dreams of a world beyond the farthest stars where they could be free. This, he felt, was such a world.

Deve turned around suddenly to face him. There was longing in her eyes—a look of wistfulness that filled him with tenderness.

"We ... we must never forget this world, Aram," she said. "Perhaps one day we can come here...." She let her voice sink low. "Oh, Aram! If we could only stay here! If we could just forget everything but this lovely, peaceful world!"

Aram Jerrold thought of Santane and the threatening clouds of war. He thought of the mighty, senseless civilization of the Thirty Suns—oblivious to the dangers that threatened to engulf it. Quite suddenly he hated it all. Hated it more than he had ever despised it when it had tortured and persecuted him. He felt trapped by his unasked-for responsibilities to the culture that had condemned him. But trapped he was, and he knew it. Even hating it, he could not let a galactic civilization vanish without trace and refuse to lift a hand to save it ... *to save something from the wreckage.*

Kant Mikal's words came back to him. Pressing, insistent, demanding.

He took Deve in his arms. "I'd want nothing more than to stay here ... with you," he said gently. "But we'd never be safe if Santane ruled the Tetrarchy. He'd never leave a paradise like this alone...."

"I know that," said Deve, sighing. "But maybe someday...." She broke off. "I'm so tired, Aram."

Jerrold thought of how long this girl had been fighting—in secret, in constant danger of her life—against the menace of an interregnum of savagery in the galaxy. It made him want to kill Santane with his bare hands and smash the Tetrarchy into cosmic rubble!

But it was no good. A responsibility had fallen onto Deve's shoulders and his. Kant Mikal had said it. And no matter how they might wish that two others had been chosen out of all the teeming billions of the Thirty Suns, both he and Deve knew that they must throw themselves between the galactic millstones and try with their last breath to avert the limbo that yawned to swallow the first stellar civilization that the race had laboriously built. It was not perfect—but it was their own.

For two days and two nights Deve and Aram waited by the restless sea of Kaidor III. They wandered over the green hills and through the wooded glades hand in hand, caught up in the wonder and beauty of the silent planet.

Aram was able to patch some of the breaks in the Serpent's hull, and together he and Deve planned what moves they must make next. Each time they left the ship, the recorders were set so that any possible word from the Star Cluster would be caught; but only the endless stream of reports and routine messages of the Thirty Suns Naval Intelligence Bureau marred the wire of the recording device when they sought the shelter of the ship again.

Together, they swam in the warm sea and rested in the sunlight on the white beach, listening to the restless sound of the ocean. It was an idyll of happiness made more poignant by the pressing nearness of danger coming ever closer.

It was on the evening of the third day on Kaidor III that the subspace radio shattered their faint hopes for the success of the Star Cluster's mission. The information came not from the Group and Kant Mikal, but viciously, shockingly, from the announcer in the Naval Intelligence sending station back on Terminus. It came, smashing the peaceful stillness of the evening calm.

"ATTENTION! ATTENTION! ALL FLEET UNITS OF THE TWENTY EIGHTH, TWENTY NINTH, AND THIRTIETH DECANT SQUADRONS! RENDEZVOUS CHECK POINT 45223 KAIDOR PROVINCE ACCORDING TO PLAN 5-25 DIRECTIVE 19-A-9! TASK FORCE COMMANDER WILL NEUTRALIZE PLANET KAIDOR FIVE FOR THE SAFETY OF THE TETRARCHY!"

Deve's face was pale. "Santane has done it at last!"

It had come, then, thought Aram heavily. The cosmic wheels were beginning to turn. A provincial governor rebelled and across light years of space forces of mind-defying magnitude began to gather. Thousands of mighty battleships, millions of men! Planet-smashing weapons! Far away, on Terminus, government bureaus shifted ponderously from peaceful administration to War. Clerks and department heads, councilmen and executives—all shifting their attentions from peacetime routines to wartime expedients. And within hours, those wartime expedients would become routine. Fixed, immutable. Routines impossible to change without painful, *time-consuming*, effort.

Jerrold spun the radio dials, searching for the government station on Kaidor V. He needed information. He needed to know what Santane was telling his population.

"... the Thirty Suns merchant vessel, Star Cluster, has fallen into our hands. The passengers and crew, sabotage agents of the Tetrarchy, have been imprisoned and will be executed ..."

The voice of the Kaidor announcer echoed menacingly through the still control room of the Serpent.

"Aram! They've got Kant Mikal and the others!" cried Deve.

"Sabotage agents!" Aram spat.

"... it is expected that the worker population will conduct itself with courage and resourcefulness under the threatened attack," continued the announcer smoothly. *"Our newly organized armed forces are even now taking measures against the tyrants' home worlds ..."*

Aram shuddered, thinking about the "measures" Santane had devised for use against the Tetrarchy. The brutalizing virus....

"... it is not to be expected that the war will be of long duration. Our scientists have developed a weapon that will make active resistance on the part of the tyrants impossible. They will not dare to attack us ..."

Confirmation, thought Aram bleakly, of Santane's dream of winning power by threats. A savage, terrible blunder!

"Generalissimo Santane has struck the shackles of the Tetrarchy from the people of Kaidor! Work and fight for victory!" The announcement was followed by the playing of martial music.

Jerrold snapped the radio off with a curse. Kant Mikal a prisoner—very likely dead already. The Fleet converging on Kaidor. Santane, drunk with power, brandishing his awful weapon over the heads of the mute billions of the Thirty Suns!

"What now, Aram?" asked Deve quietly.

"We must go to Kaidor V ... now!" he replied.

In space again, Aram tried to shake off his forebodings and failed miserably. They were speeding into a tempest of stellar magnitude, and they were but two—a man and a woman—against a war-mad galaxy.

The tiny Serpent pointed for the fifth planet of the Kaidor Sun and drew its mantle of invisibility around itself, as though to hide from the fiery stars.

Far beneath the starship, Kaidor V lay like a bright scimitar. With the energy shield momentarily off, they approached the planet's night side, deep in the global penumbra. No lights marked the populous factory cities—the world rested dark, poised to lash out against the stars, falsely confident in its possession of frightful weapons.

Carefully, Jerrold lowered the Serpent toward the spot he had marked on the planetary chart—a deep valley near Santane's capital city of Astrel. Once course and rate of descent were computed, he reactivated the energy shield and groped his way downward through the sullen night of Kaidor V.

After what seemed an eternity of waiting, Deve and Jerrold felt their ship's keel touch the ground. Aram stood by the jets, alert for the sudden tipping that would warn them that the Serpent had landed on a steep slope or crag. The deck assumed a slight angle—no more. Aram cut the power and listened to the descending whine of the gyroscopes as they coasted to a halt. Then there was silence. Only the faint hum of the energy shield broke the stillness.

Jerrold and Deve studied the chart of Kaidor V carefully. Aram had no desire to have the Serpent meet with the same fate as the ill-starred Star Cluster. Concealment and secrecy were paramount.

On the gridded chart of the planet, the dark city of Astrel lay like a blot of ink. "There is a conveyor running near here, Deve," Aram said. "It must carry ores from the mines here—" he pointed out the shafts on the map, "—to the foundries in the city. They won't be able to guard the conveyor all along its length. We can get into Astrel that way, I think."

"And what then?" asked the girl.

Jerrold shrugged. "I'm a space officer—not a spy. I know that we must try to reach Santane and help Mikal and the others if we can—"

"We had some agents still in the city," said Deve thoughtfully. "Perhaps they haven't been discovered. We can try and reach them ... they might be able to help us."

"It will be risky, Deve, now that the fight is in the open."

"I don't see how we can possibly reach Santane alone," she said.

Deve was right, of course, Aram realized. Without help they would never be able to penetrate the barriers of security the Provincial Governor must have erected between himself and the population of his planet.

Cutting the shield, Aram searched the dark landscape beyond the ports. The night was black and still. The stars made an unfamiliar pattern across the sky. A thin band of nebulosity showed the edge of the Galactic Lens in a peculiarly distorted perspective. Here, in the heart of the Thirtieth Decant, they were far from the populous worlds of the galaxy's center—farther even than they had been in Atmion Province. But this barren, cold world would be for the next few hours the center of the Thirty Suns. Here, on the metallic soil of Kaidor V, the fate of an interstellar civilization would be decided....

There were many deadly weapons in the lockers, but Jerrold decided to take only two plastic energy pistols. Such weapons would be less likely to be found by the weapons alarms that were standard street fixtures on all the planets of the Thirty Suns.

With a sigh, the valve slid open and Aram and the girl dropped to the frozen volcanic soil. The air smelled bitter, and the cold was intense. Kaidor V was more than twenty-four light-minutes from its primary, and warmth was slight. It had been chosen for the center of Kaidor Province rather than a more hospitable world because of the richness of its radioactive ores and immense nitrogen yielding deposits.

The starship had landed in a small ravine, and there, Aram decided, it could stay relatively safe from discovery. Aram marked the spot on his chart and etched it into his brain. It was hard to leave the tiny Serpent. It represented all the security they could expect on this unfriendly world.

They climbed to the crest of the ridge and dropped down onto a flat plateau, striking out across it toward the spot where Jerrold estimated they would intercept the line of the conveyor.

They walked along in silence under a canopy of oddly unfriendly stars. Presently the faint sound of machinery warned that the conveyor was near. In the darkness, they almost ran headlong into it. The light of Deve's small pocket torch revealed two belts. One bounced along empty, speeding back toward the mines in the hills; the other groaned under a heavy loading of metallic ores bound for the smelters and steel converters of Astrel.

"It's moving fast, but we'll have to jump it anyway," Aram said softly.

"Don't worry about me," replied Deve stoutly. "Just give me a hand."

Aram grinned in spite of himself. Deve's courage and resolution were a boon on this quixotic mission.

He picked her up and began to run along the uneven soil parallel to the racing conveyor. With an effort he heaved her up on to the pile of ore. He heard her give a little cry of pain as she landed among the sharp shards, and then she was gone into the blackness. Without pause, he leaped onto the belt himself, skinning his hands and legs on the rocky cargo.

For a moment he stopped to catch his breath, and then began to crawl forward toward Deve Jennet. It took him a long while to reach her, and when he did, they found that she had dropped her gun in the scramble to board the conveyor.

The thought of facing a hostile city with one small pistol did not please; but Aram realized that under no circumstances could he have hoped to out-gun the combined forces of the Thirtieth Decant, so the loss of a gun really made little difference. The whole of the Serpent's armory would do them no good if concealment failed.

"We'll have to get clear of this thing before it reaches its destination, Deve," Jerrold shouted above the roar of the belt.

"I only hope the marshalling yards and ore stockpiles aren't too well guarded!" Deve replied—and Aram silently echoed her hope.

In the near distance, coming ever nearer, were the periodic flares of the great steel converters of Astrel. The city itself seemed blacked-out, but apparently Santane—the "Generalissimo," thought Jerrold wryly—

was keeping his workers busy on weapons production right up until the last moment of danger ... another proof to Aram's mind that Santane did not believe the Tetrarchy would dare to actually attack. He must already have warned the Thirty Suns Government, perhaps sending specimens of his handiwork to impress the Supreme Council of the power of his virus weapons. Yet the Fleet would attack—Jerrold felt sure of it. The very nature of the Thirty Suns Government made any other course unthinkable. Bureaucracies, Aram knew, reacted like headless beasts to the things that threatened them, unable to make fine distinctions or true evaluations. Defiance brought reprisal. It was as simple as that.

It was difficult to see anything in the darkness, and Jerrold began to fear that they might be catapulted into the furnaces themselves. The flares in the sky seemed very close now.

A tiny blue light flashed by that Aram thought must mark the entrance to the stockpiling yards. He scrambled to his feet and pulled Deve up beside him.

"Get ready to jump clear!" he shouted in her ear.

Wind snatched at his words, and the swaying conveyor made standing difficult—almost impossible. Deve clutched at him, trying to keep her balance. And then, without warning, the belt slammed abruptly into a flat right-angle turn, pitching them off into darkness filled with hurtling chunks of ore.

Aram clung to the girl as they spilled off the belt and banged hard into a great pile of ore. More of the stuff continued to flood down on them from the conveyor above, burying them under an oppressive weight. Desperately, Jerrold clawed his way out into the open, and still clinging to Deve, rolled precipitously down the steep slope of the stockpile. They struck the bottom with bone-jarring force and lay there gasping.

A brilliant beam of light sliced through the dusty darkness, pinning them to the ore pile. Motes danced wildly in the gleaming cone. And in one awful flash of insight Aram knew what had happened ... understood the meaning of that tiny blue light he had seen. A dark-light scanner!

Floodlights came on, and the intruders found themselves blinking into a semi-circle of energy rifle muzzles in the hands of grim-faced, black-clad guards.

Aram Jerrold felt his heart sink. They were captured....

Between two files of guards, Deve and Jerrold walked into the city they had hoped to strip of its weapons. The bitterness of their failure rode hard on Jerrold's shoulders. He kept hearing again and again the phrase that Kant Mikal had used: "To save something from the wreckage...." It seemed impossible now. The giants and the furies were gathering. The might of the Thirty Suns would descend like a rain of fire on Kaidor V, and the mindless death nurtured here would sweep the inhabited worlds like a plague. The forces Jerrold had hoped to chain were free now, and threatening, like some ghastly cosmic storm. The teeming cities would crumble, the spaceways would be deserted. Night would fall on man's imperfect, but highest achievement, and he would return to the primeval muck.

Aram searched the faces of the streams of workers they passed. They were sullen, whipped men. From the tyranny of the Tetrarchy they had slipped into the clutches of Santane. For them, there was no hope, no dignity, and only the release of death could change their lot.

The black guards herded Deve and Jerrold onto a small air-sled, and the tiny craft nosed upward and into the streams of aerial traffic above the darkened city. Ahead lay the black bulk of a towering skylon. This, Aram realized, must be Santane's citadel.

The air-sled was sinking slowly to a landing on one of the many landing platforms that marred the flanks of the mighty skylon when the first alarm sirens began to wail. Aram turned his eyes to the night sky automatically. He could not hope to see the Fleet, for they must still be beyond the orbit of Kaidor X, but he did see the red streaks of the first interceptor rockets taking off. The sky in the east was greying; the attack would come by day.

The air-sled touched the landing stage, and the guards hurried Jerrold and Deve Jennet into the citadel. Through a maze of halls thronging with white-faced officers in new and unfamiliar uniforms they went, past guards and armored doorways. At last they stood in a vaulted, oblong room that hummed with activity.

It was a Combat Center. In the center of the room lay a huge, three-dimensional chart of the Thirtieth Decant and the Kaidor system. Jerrold recognized the red blips that indicated the approaching Fleet, fully ten thousand strong ... and he recognized something else too. He had felt this kind of tension in ships of the Navy. It was fear—universal, jittery fear. These people, Aram knew suddenly, were terribly, desperately afraid of that advancing armada. Their leader had told them that it would not dare attack, yet it came on inexorably and they were afraid.

Yellow streaks in the chart showed the track of interceptors, already fanning out from Kaidor V, seeking targets in the huge, onrushing formation of mighty battleships that spread across light-minutes of space. The tiny weapons had already taken a small toll of the slower Fleet vessels, but the rest continued sunward, their losses unfelt.

This was what Aram feared Santane would not or could not realize ... that no matter how dreadful his virus weapon, forces of such magnitude could not be halted by threats once they were put in motion.

Now Santane's secretly built fleet was blasting into space. Jerrold estimated that it consisted of perhaps five hundred large starships—torpedo launchers mainly, built for defense.

Near Kaidor VII, the ringed giant, the two Fleets made first contact. The battle of the Thirtieth Decant had begun.

The guards shoved at Jerrold, and he was led away from the chart and its fascinating picture of battle. He and Deve were taken up a spiralling staircase to the balcony that overlooked the Combat Center and through a heavily guarded door.

The chamber in which they now found themselves was strangely quiet after the fear-tinged confusion of the Combat Center. All but one of their guards withdrew, and Aram faced a tall, powerfully built man who stood engrossed in a bank of scanner-views of the battle.

Presently the man looked up to scowl at his prisoners. Aram Jerrold knew at once that it was—at last—Santane.

Aram studied the man with interest. Here was the man whose rebellion had catapulted the galaxy into war. Because of Santane, billions faced degradation or extinction. It seemed impossible that one man could cause such a cataclysmic upheaval in a star-spanning culture. But there was more to it than that, of course. Santane—as a man—was simply one more bit of protoplasm in the vast mystery of the cosmos. But Santane—as a symbol— was real and important. He was a living monument to the immutable face that tyranny begets more tyranny, and that the very existence of absolute power results in the two awful corollaries ... ambition and strife.

The Tetrarchy had spawned Santane just as surely as night follows day. Santane was the cancer in the body of the despotism of the Thirty Suns that was destined to destroy it ... and, thought Aram grimly, himself with it.

Aram Jerrold studied the craggy face and the deep-set, glowing eyes as Santane stood there before the simulacrum of Armageddon in the scanners, and knew there was madness in the man.

Santane spoke, and the sound rasped across the senses.

"You are Aram Jerrold and Deve Jennet—agents of the Tetrarchy. Spies ... high ranking spies!" His icy gaze searched the faces of the man and woman before him. "Do you deny it?"

"We are who you say," replied Jerrold evenly, "but we are not spies. The Tetrarchy has undoubtedly set a price on our heads by now."

"You lie! The Tetrarchy sent you here because they are afraid of me." Santane laughed scornfully, "They have seen what I can do."

"Don't be a fool, Santane," Jerrold said softly. "The Tetrarchy is not afraid of you. It can't be. It hasn't the ability to fear you or anything else. Can't you see that?" He indicated the scanners. The Fleet was bearing ever closer to Kaidor V, slashing through the cordons of defensive craft doggedly, impervious to losses and dying ships and men.

Fear touched Santane's face ... but for just an instant. Aram knew with sinking heart that the man's madness would not let him believe the truth.

"No," said Santane tensely. "They are afraid of me—or you wouldn't have been sent here."

Aram was struck with a sudden, grotesque pity for the man. All the weeks he had spent in danger and in preparation for this mission that had failed, he had thought of Santane as the living incarnation of crafty evil. What he saw before him now was a insane man—frightened by the mighty forces he had unleashed and could not now turn or control. In that moment, Aram felt that Kant Mikal's injunction to save something from the ruins was truly impossible, for nothing could come right when a single madman could smash in days the work of millennia.

Santane's face was again rigid and cold. "Perhaps you have not seen what my biological weapons can do.... Guard! Bring in the others!"

Aram felt an icy hand closing about his heart. The others....

Kant Mikal ... the men and women of the Star Cluster....

"Santane ... you haven't...!" Jerrold broke off in horror as the guard returned, leading a line of five shambling beasts. The creatures fought the chains that bound them, howling with outrage.

"How," demanded Santane, "can Terminus attack me if they face *that*?" His eyes lit, kindled with some obscene pleasure at the spectacle. "First there are pains in the neck and head. Blinding—agonizing pains! Then comes unconsciousness, and memory goes ... then the glands alter, and men become ... beasts...."

Deve Jennet moaned. Her friends and comrades were in that line of disfigured subhuman things. She clutched at Aram for support.

Jerrold felt red fury explode within him. He wanted to feel his bare hands on Santane's throat ... his teeth in his flesh. With an oath he launched himself bodily at the smiling madman, hands groping for the throat under the twisted grin. He saw Santane back away in sudden fright, and the black flash of the guard interposing himself between them. The guard raised his rifle and brought the muzzle down in a chopping arc. Aram felt a searing pain above his eyes and pitched into a reddish blur of oblivion....

Jerrold awoke in a small, glassed-in chamber. His head ached dully, and he could feel the stiffness of dried blood on his brow. He rolled over and staggered to his feet, realizing that he must be at the very pinnacle of the mighty skylon that housed Santane's headquarters.

The same black guard who had struck him down stood impassive in the corner, and Aram could see Santane standing with Deve on a small landing stage beyond the glass. He saw something else, too, and his breath came faster. There was a small air-sled on the landing stage, bright with new paint and Santane's own insigne of the Trident and Flame.

There was a subspace radio installation in the corner of the aerie, and Aram Jerrold knew instantly that he had been brought up to the skylon's top to establish contact with the invading Fleet, to warn the forces of the Thirty Suns to surrender.

Santane returned with Deve held at his side. The sight of the man's hand possessively on Deve's wrist brought a return of Aram's fury.

"You see," Santane said with a thin smile, "the Fleet *does* fear me. They have broken off their attack and are circling beyond the stratosphere."

That meant, Aram knew, that the ships of the Thirty Suns were preparing for bombardment of Kaidor V. Knowing the richness of the nitrogen-bearing surface soil of the planet, the Task Force commander would undoubtedly be readying his vessels to rain down nitrogen fission bombs, trying to exceed critical mass in the air and ground of the planet and setting off chain reactions to rip it apart by the expenditure of the energy contained in the globe itself. Santane, not being a space officer, could not know that.

Kant Mikal's wish to have something saved from the wreckage now could be accomplished in only two ways—both impossible to Aram's mind.

He and Deve could escape, and save themselves ... or he could prevent Santane from launching his interstellar missiles when the bombs began to fall.

"Call the Fleet commander," Santane ordered brusquely. "Tell him he must land and place himself at my orders."

Such a call would be ignored. Aram knew that....

"Hurry!" Santane demanded pettishly.

Still Aram could bring himself to no decision.

Santane turned, took a stoppered vial from a cabinet and faced Aram again with a scowl. "One drop of this on the skin, and a human being becomes ... what you saw below. Shall I use it on the woman to convince you where your duty lies?"

Aram felt his heart skip a beat. Santane was not bluffing. Pressed, he would carry out his threat from sheer perverted malice. Aram looked hungrily toward the small air-sled on the landing....

He took a step toward the radio. Very probably his voice, recognized, would brings the bombs even quicker—but there was no way to convince Santane of that. He was beyond reason.

A high pitched sound broke the stillness. Aram pitched instinctively to the floor as a bomb struck the ground far below and near the base of the skylon! The whole structure shook with the force of the concussion, the glass of the aerie fogging into a maze of tiny cracks. Fragments of the ceiling came powdering down. Santane staggered against the wall, the vial still in his hand, a look of terrified disbelief on his face.

"*No!*" he gasped. "*They wouldn't dare....*"

Aram tried to reach Deve's side, but Santane was quicker.

"Tell them to call off the attack!" he screamed, "or I infect the woman! Quickly! Quickly!"

Aram spun on his knee and dived for Santane. The vial flew across the room and shattered against the wall. Jerrold smashed his fist into Santane's distorted face—he felt the splintering of teeth in the shattered mouth. A sizzling beam of fire flashed past Aram's eyes. He straightened and struck Santane again, sending the man staggering across the room.

Jerrold smashed his fist into Santane's distorted face....

Instead of attacking or trying to escape, Santane leaped for a wall communicator. His battered face was a mask of maniacal rage. Jerrold caught him but ... too late to prevent four words from screeching into the microphone....

"Fire the virus missiles!"

Aram sobbed with frustrated rage and swung his clenched fists again and again into Santane's bloody face. He rolled on the littered floor, trying to strangle the life from the wildly struggling madman who had spawned disaster.

Another bomb fell, rocking the skylon. Beams clattered down from the towering superstructure, caving in sections of the aerie's roof. The guard, who had been circling for a safe shot at Aram, shrieked in agony as a metal section took him across the shoulders and snapped his back like a twig.

Suddenly Aram felt a wetness on his clothes and a bitterness on his tongue. The two wrestling men had rolled into the pool of liquid from the broken-vial.

Santane screamed with terror, and in a frantic burst of energy, broke away and stumbled out onto the landing stage and the air-sled.

Deve rushed to Aram, helping him to his feet. As she touched him, he recoiled.

"Don't, Deve! Don't touch me!"

But the girl's hands, too, were wet with the sticky stuff of the vial, and Aram knew with a sick certainty that they were both infected with the virus of bestiality.

"After *him!*" Hopeless now, sick with despair, Aram wanted only to kill Santane.

But Santane had not launched the air-sled. Instead he knelt on its deck, a medical kit in his hands. He was trying with trembling fingers to fill a syringe from a narrow capsule. Jerrold knocked the instrument from his hands and dragged him from the machine. The madman fought back with desperate strength, but Aram smashed him again and again against the stones of the landing. In a last spasmodic effort, Santane caught Aram by the throat and forced him toward the edge. Far below, the glowing, radioactive smoke of death roiled against the sides of the weakened skylon. Aram could see flames eating ravenously at the lower levels. Santane shrieked with triumph as Aram hung momentarily over the abyss. Aram twisted....

And then Santane was gone, vanishing in a long wailing fall, twisting and turning like a rag-doll until his scream of terror blended with the cry of another falling bomb.

Without pausing to catch his breath, Jerrold returned to the air-sled and picked up the syringe. It was only partly full, and the capsule that Santane had used to load it had been smashed. It was the antidote ... it had to be the antidote!

"Deve, here!" With shaking hands he caught her arm and sank the needle into her flesh, squeezing the plunger down. As the fluid in the cylinder reached the half-way point, Deve pulled away.

"That's enough! The rest is for you," she breathed.

"No, Deve! I don't know if it's enough for both of us. Santane was going to take the full measure for himself, and he should know...."

Deve Jennet shook her head. "I don't care," she said. "I wouldn't want to go on ... without you."

Aram pleaded but Deve would not be convinced. She had no wish to survive alone. Finally, Aram took the syringe and emptied it into his forearm.

"Now, we'll see," he muttered.

The howl of bombs was a steady, increasing cacophony now, and, though ships of Santane's fleet still fought, the Thirty Suns naval force bombed almost at will. The skylon shook and buckled under the bombardment and the radiation count on the counters in the wrecked aerie showed an increasingly dangerous concentration. Still the virus missiles took the air, streaking the radioactive clouds with their tail-flares, and Aram watched with sick horror as the awful spawn of the Kaidor Sun rose to spread bestiality while he stood helplessly by.

"Aram," Deve spoke to him gently amid the rising symphony of destruction. "We have to get clear, Aram. Remember what Kant Mikal said ... and we are all that's left now."

"The Fleet...."

"The Fleet will return to Terminus. We can't stop them," Deve said with finality.

Aram knew it was true. Mindless to the last, the bureaucracy would stick to its directives and general orders. The Fleet would return ... to oblivion.

They mounted the air-sled and slanted up into the tortured air of the dying planet. A huge starship with the golden Spaceship and Sun blazon came hurtling down out of the sky like a fiery brand, a smaller ship bearing Santane's Trident and Flame imbedded in its flank. The two ships dissolved into a ball of greasy fire as they smashed into the crowded buildings of shattered Astrel.

More and more nitrogen fission bombs were falling now as the air-sled streaked across the flaming sky toward the ravine that hid the Serpent. The very soil of the planet seemed to dance in a hellish carnival of destruction. Glancing back, Aram saw the towering skylon come plunging down in torrents of rubble and human flesh. He knew with finality that he was witnessing the end of everything he had known—the chaotic collapse of a culture that had spawned its own nemesis. Man—diving from the pinnacle of stellar dominion to the depths of nothingness ... because he had tolerated tyranny.

Jerrold shook his head to clear away the sudden pain that stabbed across his temples. One thought grew in his mind with increasing clarity. He and Deve must somehow survive. Perhaps other men and women would come through the end in remote worlds, but there was no way of being certain. He had to be sure ... he had to know that the end would not come for all the race. He, a man, and Deve, a woman, could still carry out the mercifully dead Kant Mikal's injunction. In those fleeting moments above the writhing, doomed surface of Kaidor V, survival became an obsession with Aram Jerrold.

The Serpent awaited them where they had left it, and they hurried through the valve, feeling the tremblors of the fifth planet's death agonies.

Aram drove the ship upward, seeking the safety of space and their haven. Both knew where they were going, though neither had put it into words.

At a distance of five diameters from the globe of Kaidor V, Aram paused to see the death of a world.

Like a savage animal, the Fleet continued to worry the trembling planet with a vicious hail of bombs. The pair in the Serpent could see bright internal fires as the crust of the world split under the hideous attack. Like a stricken thing, Kaidor V seemed to totter on its axis. Great chunks of rock were blown clear by the pressure of expanding inner fires.

For hours, the death agonies of the planet continued, until finally, like a bursting bubble, the globe expanded. Huge slashes appeared from pole to pole. The ice caps vanished into twin clouds of superheated steam. Fragments peeled off as gravitational balances were disturbed. Globules of molten lava fanned out, like strings of beads. Kaidor V trembled with a cosmic delirium—great prominences of atomic fire leaping far into space. And then, quite suddenly, it was over. With its heart ripped out by the violent fission of its inner substance, the hollow shell collapsed into a swirling, nebulous cloud of cosmic rubble, rapidly spreading out into a belt of tiny planetoids spanning the place where once a mighty world circled the parent star....

The Serpent settled softly into a wooded glade and grew still. Within, Aram Jerrold fought the wracking pains in his head, screaming aloud with the agony of it. Deve lay unconscious on the steel deck, moaning softly.

Aram knew that the antidote he had injected into their veins was not enough. Vaguely, he recalled that once—long ago, it seemed—he had been told that a small amount of specific would prevent physical damage. But the virus was claiming him, nonetheless. The pounding agony in his head was streaked with delirious phantasms. Kant Mikal's words echoed through his brain, though he no longer recognized them as other than his own. His screaming madness took the shape of those words as he lifted Deve in his arms and staggered out of the ship.

Driven by some deep seated racial memory, he stumbled toward the sea—the mother—the giver of life. The sheer brutal agony of the virus increased with every step, blinding him with its intensity, until at last he could bear it no longer and sank to his knees on the white sand of a beach and pitched forward across the still form of the woman he carried, hands outstretched toward the shallows of a restless sea that laved him ... laved him....

Deve stood nude in the glory of the morning sunlight and lifted her arms to the sky in an ecstacy of freedom. "How lovely it is," she murmured.

The figure at her feet stirred and she touched him playfully with a bare foot.

Aram woke, puzzled. Something, deep in the back of his mind troubled him. There had been something....

"Come swim with me!"

Aram looked up at the naked girl before him. She was Deve. He knew that. He tried to remember more, but he could not. A strange shroud seemed to have covered up everything ... language he seemed to command, but....

He put the troublesome thoughts out of his mind and stripped off the strange coverings on his body. Hand in hand with Deve, he waded into the sea. They swam and played in the warm sunlight, and presently, tiring of their sport, sought the shade of a wooded glade.

As they walked hand in hand among the flowering shrubs under the trees, Deve stopped abruptly.

"Aram," she said, puzzled, "what is that?"

An alien shape stood among the verdure, gleaming where the sunlight pierced the foliage. It was a long cylinder, tapered at both ends and lined with round, blank ports. They stood there staring at the spaceship with perplexed incomprehension. Both had a vague feeling that it was familiar.

"What is it, Aram?" the girl asked again.

"I ... don't know," he confessed.

"I think we did know ... once," Deve said softly. "Aram, why are we here?"

Why? The question touched off sparks of memory that brightened and as quickly faded. Aram spoke, painfully dredging the words from beyond the veil of forgetfulness.

"We ... must ... save ... something ... from the ruins."

"What ruins?" the girl asked impatiently. "What is it we must save?"

But memory had faded. Aram could not answer her.

Still she persisted with feminine curiosity unsatisfied.

"Aram, what is this place?"

For a long moment he stood in silence beside her in the sun-splashed glade. He listened to the gentle sound of the wind in the trees and the restless murmur of the sea. Presently he replied, but with a question. "Are you happy here, Deve?"

"Oh, yes!" she breathed.

He took her in his arms, the spaceship and the past completely forgotten.

"Then this is ... Paradise," he said.

EPILOGUE

... And twenty thousand years after, as Man reached again for the stars ... these two lived in memory ... as *Adam and Eve*.